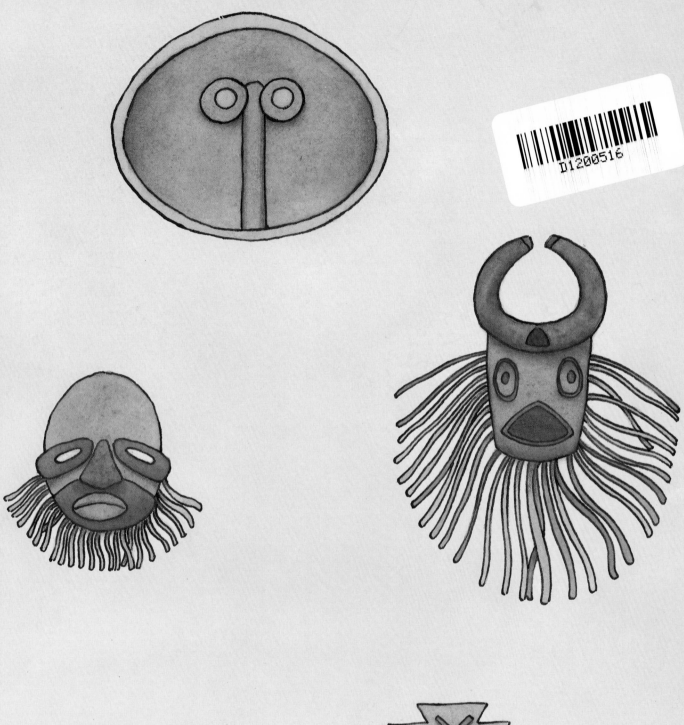
D1200516

First published in French as Edmond et le grand singe
by l'ecole des loisirs, Paris, France.
Copyright © 1991 by l'ecole des loisirs.
English translation copyright © 1992 by Tambourine Books.

All rights reserved. No part of this book may be reproduced
or utilized in any form or by any means, electronic or mechanical,
including photocopying, recording, or by any information
storage or retrieval system, without permission in writing from
the Publisher. Inquiries should be addressed to Tambourine Books,
a division of William Morrow & Company, Inc.,
1350 Avenue of the Americas, New York, New York 10019.
Printed in Italy.

Library of Congress Cataloging-in-Publication Data
Léonard, Alain, 1961- [Edmond et le grand singe. English]
Barnaby and the big gorilla/by Alain Léonard.—1st U.S. ed.
p. cm.
Translation of: Edmond et le grand singe.
Summary: A little boy comes to terms with the big gorilla
at his uncle's house.
ISBN 0-688-11291-9 (trade) — (0-688-11292-7 (lib.)
[1. Gorillas—Fiction.] I. Title.
PZ7.L54274Bar 1992 [E]—dc20 91-25414 CIP AC

1 3 5 7 9 10 8 6 4 2
First U.S. edition 1992

BARNABY and the BIG GORILLA

by Alain Léonard

Tambourine Books  New York

At Barnaby's uncle's house there is a big gorilla.

It's huge and furry and has big teeth. It scares Barnaby.

Barnaby doesn't go near the gorilla. He thinks it is so big it could swallow ten little rabbits just like him.

"Don't be afraid," explains his uncle, "it won't bite you."

However, as soon as Barnaby's uncle turns his back, the gorilla opens its mouth and bares its teeth.

"It's alive," cries Barnaby. But his uncle is too busy to pay attention.

One day Barnaby's horse rolls under the big gorilla's paws.

"Go away," cries Barnaby, "I want to get my horse."

But the gorilla won't leave.

So Barnaby tries to trick the gorilla. He makes a dummy of himself, puts it on a skateboard, and hides behind a shield.

Unfortunately the trick doesn't work. The big gorilla must be very clever.

Next Barnaby tries to push it with a stick.

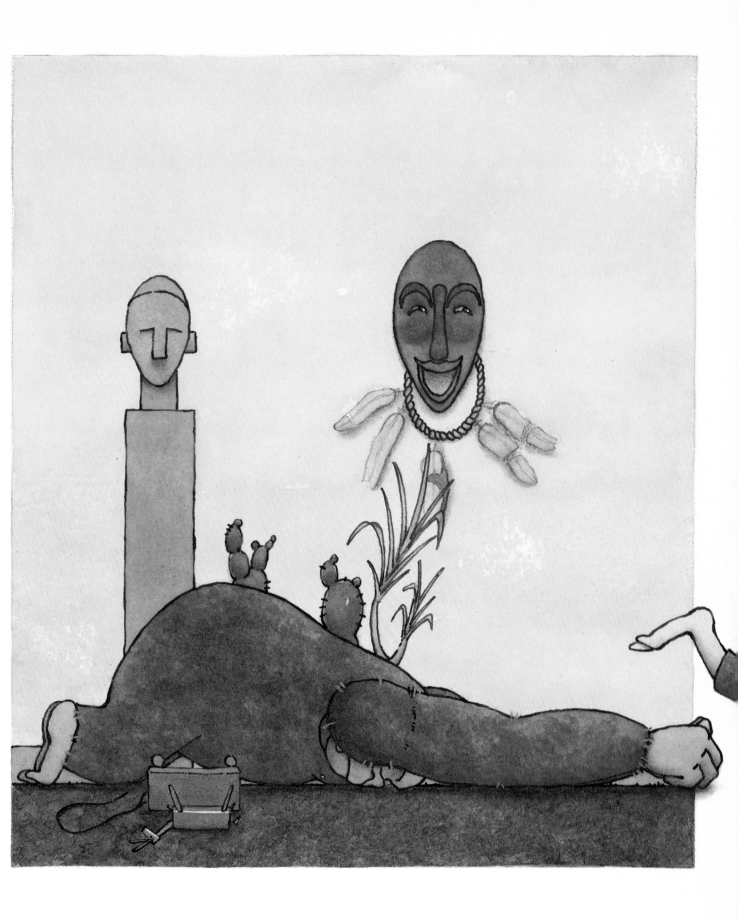

But the big gorilla lunges toward him.

When Barnaby returns the gorilla is still on the floor and Barnaby's uncle picks it up. Barnaby still does not have his horse.

"That's it!" Barnaby thinks, "I'm going to get back my horse, right now!"

Bravely he marches toward the big gorilla.

At last Barnaby has won. "I am very strong," he declares.